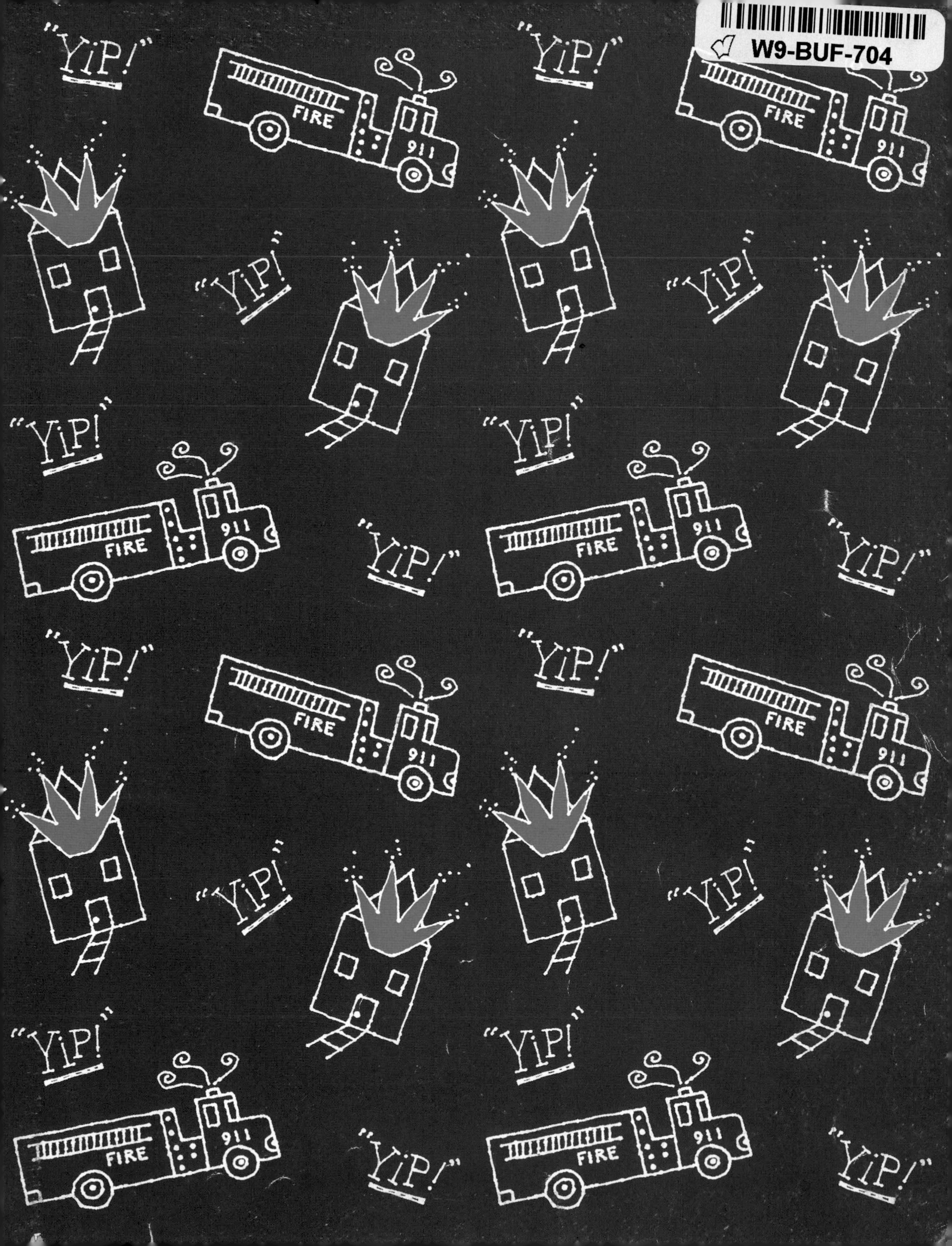
"YiP!"
FIRE
911

To Caleb Back

HOLIDAY HOUSE is registered in the U.S. Patent and
Trademark Office.
Printed and Bound in April 2013 at
Tien Wah Press, Johor Bahru, Johor, Malaysia.
The text typeface is Report School.
The artwork was rendered with
gouache on illustration board.
www.holidayhouse.com
First Edition
1 3 5 7 9 10 8 6 4 2

Library of Congress Cataloging-in-Publication Data
Reed, Lynn Rowe.
Fireman Fred / Lynn Rowe Reed. — 1st ed.
p. cm. — (I like to read)
Summary: Follows Fred as he speeds to a fire,
performs a rescue, and makes a new friend.
ISBN 978-0-8234-2658-4 (hardcover)
[1. Fire fighters—Fiction.] I. Title.
PZ7.R25273Fir 2013   [E]—dc23   2012000017

FIREMAN FRED

Lynn Rowe Reed

Holiday House / New York

Fireman Fred naps.

The bell rings.

"Run! Run," calls the chief.

"Get on," yells Fred.

The truck races.

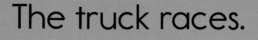

The horn honks.

"Help!" says the lady.
The fire hisses.

"Yip," says the dog.

"Get the hose,"
says the chief.

"Done!" Fred calls.

"Help! Help," yells the lady.
"Mew, mew," says the cat.

"Yours?" asks Fred.
"Mine," says the lady.

"Yip," says
the dog.

"Yours?" asks Fred.
"No!" they call.
"No! No! No!"

"Alone?" asks Fred.
"Yip," says the dog.

"Home!" calls the chief.

FIRE

They are back.
Fred can nap.

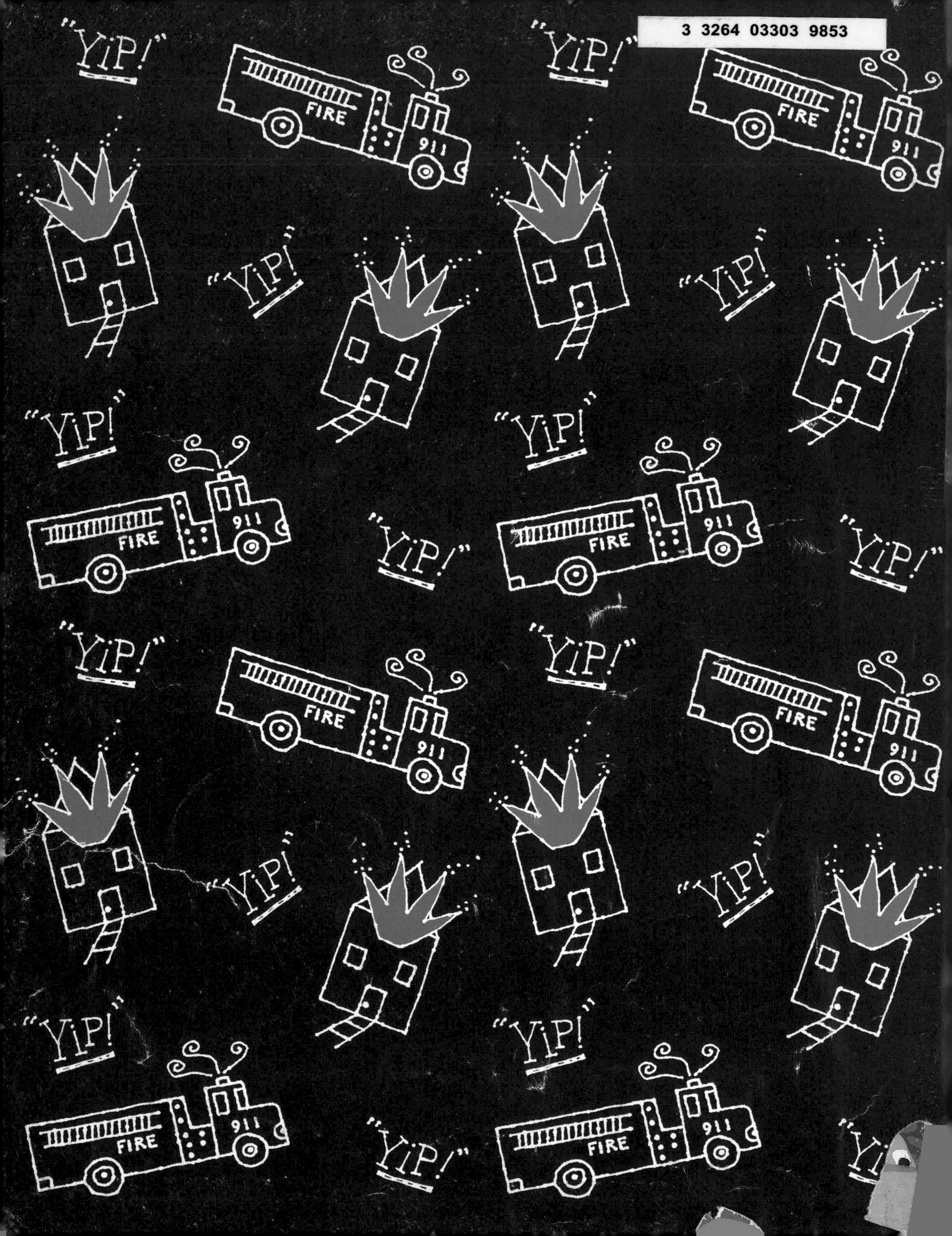
"YiP!"
FIRE
911

THERE'S A HOLE IN THE LOG

IN THE

LOG

ON THE BOTTOM OF THE LAKE

LOREN LONG

PHILOMEL BOOKS

"Do you hear voices?"

THERE'S A **LOG** ON THE BOTTOM OF THE LAKE.
THERE'S A **LOG** ON THE BOTTOM OF THE LAKE.

THERE'S A LOG? THERE'S A LOG!

"It's just a piece of rotten wood."

THERE'S A LOG LOG LOG
THERE'S A LOG ON THE BOTTOM OF THE LAKE.

THERE'S A **HOLE** IN THE **LOG** ON THE BOTTOM OF THE LAKE.
THERE'S A **HOLE** IN THE **LOG** ON THE BOTTOM OF THE LAKE.

"A whole what? It just looks empty to me."

THERE'S A HOLE? THERE'S A HOLE!

THERE'S A **HOLE HOLE HOLE**
IN THE **LOG LOG LOG**

THERE'S A **HOLE** IN THE **LOG**
ON THE **BOTTOM OF THE LAKE**.

"Dial 911! Turtle on its back! Emergency! Turtle freaking out!"

THERE'S A FROG IN THE HOLE IN THE LOG ON THE BOTTOM OF THE LAKE.

THERE'S A **FROG** IN THE **HOLE**
IN THE **LOG** ON THE BOTTOM OF THE LAKE.

"Hey, look!
It's the guys.
Wait for us!"

THERE'S A FROG?
THERE'S A FROG!

THERE'S A FROG FROG FROG IN THE HOLE HOLE HOLE IN THE LOG LOG LOG

THERE'S A FROG IN THE HOLE IN THE LOG ON THE BOTTOM OF THE LAKE.

"Please just try to fit in this time. NO MORE SNAIL TALK!"

THERE'S A HAIR ON THE FROG IN THE HOLE IN THE LOG ON THE BOTTOM OF THE LAKE.

THERE'S A **HAIR** ON THE **FROG** IN THE **HOLE** IN THE **LOG** ON THE BOTTOM OF THE LAKE.

"Okay, I get it. Now you're too cool for school. Well, don't forget Mr. Turtle back here!"

THERE'S A HAIR?
THERE'S A HAIR!

"Ew. Is there really a hair on that frog?"

THERE'S A HAIR HAIR HAIR
ON THE FROG FROG FROG
IN THE HOLE HOLE HOLE
IN THE LOG LOG LOG

THERE'S A HAIR ON THE FROG IN THE HOLE IN THE LOG ON THE BOTTOM OF THE LAKE.

"It gets worse. His hair has bugs."

THERE'S A **FLY** ON THE **HAIR** ON THE **FROG** IN THE **HOLE** IN THE **LOG** ON THE BOTTOM OF THE LAKE.

THERE'S A FLY?
THERE'S A FLY!

"Oh, great! I'll never get this song out of my head."

THERE'S A GNAT ON THE FLY ON THE HAIR ON THE FROG IN THE HOLE IN THE LOG ON THE BOTTOM OF THE LAKE.

"Ugh, now his bug has bugs?"

THERE'S A **GNAT** ON THE **FLY** ON THE **HAIR** ON THE **FROG** IN THE **HOLE** IN THE **LOG** ON THE BOTTOM OF THE LAKE.

THERE'S A GNAT?
THERE'S A GNAT!

THERE'S A GNAT GNAT GNAT
ON THE FLY FLY FLY
ON THE HAIR HAIR HAIR
ON THE FROG FROG FROG
IN THE HOLE HOLE HOLE
IN THE LOG LOG LOG

THERE'S A GNAT ON THE FLY ON THE
HAIR ON THE FROG IN THE
HOLE IN THE LOG
ON THE BOTTOM OF THE LAKE.

"This place is weird.
I'm out of here!"

THERE'S A **FISH** NEAR THE **GNAT** ON THE **FLY** ON THE **HAIR** ON THE **FROG** IN THE **HOLE** IN THE **LOG** ON THE BOTTOM OF THE LAKE.

THERE'S A **FISH** NEAR THE **GNAT** ON THE **FLY** ON THE **HAIR** ON THE **FROG** IN THE **HOLE** IN THE **LOG** ON THE BOTTOM OF THE LAKE.

"Uh-oh..."

THERE'S A . . .

UH-OH.

CHOMP, SNAP, GULP!

THERE'S A FISH ON THE BOTTOM OF THE LAKE.
THERE'S A FISH ON THE BOTTOM OF THE LAKE.
THERE'S A FISH?
JUST A FISH.
THERE'S A FISH ON THE BOTTOM OF THE LAKE . . .

There's a Hole in the Log on the Bottom of the Lake

VERSE 1

There's a log on the bottom of the lake.
There's a log on the bottom of the lake.
There's a LOG? There's a LOG!
There's a log log log
There's a log on the bottom of the lake.

VERSE 2

There's a hole in the log on the bottom of the lake.
There's a hole in the log on the bottom of the lake.
There's a HOLE? There's a HOLE!
There's a hole hole hole
    in the log log log
There's a hole in the log on the bottom of the lake.

VERSE 3

There's a frog in the hole in the log on the bottom of the lake.
There's a frog in the hole in the log on the bottom of the lake.
There's a FROG? There's a FROG!
There's a frog frog frog
    in the hole hole hole
    in the log log log
There's a frog in the hole in the log on the bottom of the lake.

VERSE 4

There's a hair on the frog in the hole in the log on the bottom
    of the lake.
There's a hair on the frog in the hole in the log on the bottom
    of the lake.
There's a HAIR? There's a HAIR!
There's a hair hair hair
    on the frog frog frog
    in the hole hole hole
    in the log log log
There's a hair on the frog in the hole in the log on the bottom
    of the lake.

VERSE 5

There's a fly on the hair on the frog in the hole in the log on
    the bottom of the lake.
There's a fly on the hair on the frog in the hole in the log on
    the bottom of the lake.
There's a FLY? There's a FLY!
There's a fly fly fly
    on the hair hair hair
    on the frog frog frog
    in the hole hole hole
    in the log log log
There's a fly on the hair on the frog in the hole in the log on
    the bottom of the lake.

VERSE 6

There's a gnat on the fly on the hair on the frog in the hole in
    the log on the bottom of the lake.
There's a gnat on the fly on the hair on the frog in the hole in
    the log on the bottom of the lake.
There's a GNAT? There's a GNAT!
There's a gnat gnat gnat
    on the fly fly fly
    on the hair hair hair
    on the frog frog frog
    in the hole hole hole
    in the log log log
There's a gnat on the fly on the hair on the frog in the hole in
    the log on the bottom of the lake.

VERSE 7

There's a fish near the gnat on the fly on the hair on the frog in
    the hole in the log on the bottom of the lake.
There's a fish near the gnat on the fly on the hair on the frog in
    the hole in the log on the bottom of the lake.
There's a . . . Uh-oh.
CHOMP, SNAP, GULP!
There's a fish on the bottom of the lake.
There's a fish on the bottom of the lake.
There's a FISH? Just a FISH.
There's a fish on the bottom of the lake . . .

"For some reason, now I have the urge to take guitar lessons."